THE THREE LITTLE HAWAIIAN PIGS AND THE MAGIC SHARK

By Donivee Martin Laird
Illustrated by Carol Jossem

Barnaby Books Honolulu, Hawaii

Also by Barnaby Books:

Hau Kea and the Seven Menehune
    (Snow White and the Seven Dwarfs)
Keaka and the Liliko'i Vine
    (Jack and the Beanstalk)
'Ula Li'i and the Magic Shark
    (Little Red Riding Hood)
Wili Wai Kula and the Three Mongooses
    (Goldilocks and the Three Bears)

From the Maile Collection published by Barnaby Books
    Māui and His Magical Deeds
by Kats Kajiyama

Published by:
Barnaby Books, Inc.
3290 Pacific Heights Road
Honolulu, Hawaii 96813

Printed and bound in China under the direction of:
KWA Communications, Inc. and Everbest Printing

Library of Congress Catalog Number 81-67047

ISBN 0-940350-25-4

Twelfth Printing, 10/02

Our aloha
to
Sara, Leah, Thaddeus,
Joey and Adam

PRONUNCIATION GUIDE

The 12 letters in the Hawaiian alphabet are:
A, E, H, I, K, L, M, N, O, P, U, W

consonants
H, K, L, M, N, P are pronounced as in English
W is usually pronounced as V

vowels
A like a in farm
E like e in set
I like y in pretty

O like o in hold
U like oo in soon

plural
As there is no S in Hawaiian, the plural is formed by word usage or the addition of another word such as nā to the sentence.

One morning in Hawaii
a mother and father pig
called their children together.

"Our dear pua'a keiki," they said with sorrow
in their voices, "as much as we love you, it is time for you
to become grown-ups and seek your own way in the world.
Here is a sack of money for each of you. Spend it wisely and
always be careful of strangers."

After saying aloha to their parents, the three little pigs set off down the road looking forward to a life full of happiness, adventure, and riches.

They had gone only a short distance when
they met a man with a load of pili grass.
"Ah ha," said the first little pig. "This is for me.
I will build myself a grass house and live beside the sea."

So, he bought the pili grass and happily headed towards the beach where he built his house. It was finished quickly and he took his pole, his net, his small bucket for opihi, and he went fishing.

The other two little pigs
went on until they met a
man selling driftwood.

"Ah ha," said the second
little pig. "This is for
me. I will build myself
a house of driftwood and
live beside the sea."

Feeling pleased with himself, he quickly built
his house and went to join the first little pig
fishing and scraping opihi off the slippery rocks.

The third little pig went on until he met a man selling lava rock. "Ah ha," said the third little pig. "This is for me. I will build myself a house of lava rock and live beside the sea and go fishing with my brothers." It took many days to build the house and before it was done, one brother came to visit the third little pig.

"Why are you wasting your time on such a hard house to build?" he asked. "We are pau with our houses and have time to fish and take it easy surfing and playing. Forget this house, come with us." The third little pig just shook his head and said he would rather take his time and build a strong house.

After many days of hard work,
the lava rock house was finished.
It was sturdy and strong and the
third little pig was pleased
with his work. He checked his
doors and windows carefully
to be sure his house was snug
and safe.

Then off he went to join
his brothers beside the sea.

The three little pigs threw their nets
and pulled in reef creatures like the
brilliant yellow tang, the horned humuhumu, or
the slimy octopus, heʻe. They climbed over the
wet rocks scraping off the delicious opihi and
once in a while they caught puhi paka,
the fierce fanged eel.

Sometimes they took their poles, and standing far out on the rocks, fished the deeper waters for the larger ulua, opakapaka, and ahi. They played tag, splashed in the tide pools, and chased tiny sand crabs. Their days were clear and sunny, and cooled by gentle trade winds.

When the waves broke just right
beside the reef, they took their
surfboards and caught long
breathtaking rides to the beach.

Meanwhile, an evil magic shark watched them from
deep down where the water is green. Back and forth swam
the magic shark, his long teeth shining in the gloomy water.
He especially wanted to eat the three little pigs
since they looked so sweet and tender.

He knew he couldn't catch them on the rocks, for
the lava was sharp and the pigs too quick. He wished
they would fall off their surfboards, but the pigs
were too good and went too fast through the rough water.

So, watching and planning, the magic shark drooled and thought of the yummy little pigs.

One morning, unable to stand
his craving any longer,
the magic shark disguised
himself as a shave ice man
and knocked on the door of
the first little pig's house.

"Little Pig,
Little Pig,
let me
come in,"
he called.
"I have
plenty
shave ice!"

The little pig peeked out of the window. He was hot and thirsty and the cool, colorful shave ice looked so tasty. He grabbed his money and started to open the door.

But, just in time, he saw a fin on the shave ice man's back and he knew it was really the magic shark. He quickly shut and locked the door. The shark knocked harder and called, "Little Pig, Little Pig, let me come in." "Oh no," cried the little pig. "Not by the hair on my chinny, chin, chin."

The magic shark was hot and hungry
and the little pig's answer made him very
mad. He yelled, "Little Pig, Little Pig,
let me come in or I will huff and I will
puff and I will blow your house down."
The little pig did not open his door.
(After all he wasn't crazy, he knew what
the magic shark wanted.) So, the very mad
magic shark huffed and the very mad
magic shark puffed and the very mad
magic shark blew down the first
little pig's house.

The first little pig ran out
of the back door and down the path to the house
of the second little pig. The very mad magic shark went
back to the ocean to cool off and make a new plan.

In a few days, the magic shark was hungry for little pigs again. This time he dressed up as a beachboy, wearing white pants, a coconut leaf hat, and a lei around his neck. He knocked on the door of the second little pig's house and called, "Little Pig, Little Pig, let's talk story and play ukes." The little pigs grabbed their ukulele and nose flute and opened the door. The beachboy smiled and the little pigs saw rows and rows of long, sharp white teeth and just in time, they slammed the door.

"Little Pig, Little Pig, let me come in," called the hot
and hungry magic shark anxiously.
"Oh no," cried the little pigs. (They knew that was no
friendly beachboy out on the steps.)
"Not by the hairs on our chinny, chin, chins."

This made the magic shark upset so
he roared, "Then I will huff and I will
puff and I will blow your house down."
Just as he said he would, the very upset
magic shark huffed and the very upset
magic shark puffed and the very upset
magic shark blew down the house of the
second little pig.

The little pig and his brother
jumped out of the window and ran down
the path to the house of the third
little pig.

Once more the magic shark, hot and still hungry, swam angrily down to his watery home to plot and scheme. After a few days his hunger pangs were so bad that the magic shark decided to try again.

This time he went pretending to be a lei seller. He knocked on the third little pig's door and called sweetly, "Little Pig, Little Pig, let me come in. I have leis to sell." The three little pigs loved to wear leis and were happy to hear a sweet voice calling.

They looked out and saw the lei seller in her mu'u mu'u and lauhala hat, with flower leis on her arms. But then, they also saw a shark's tail sticking out from under the mu'u mu'u. They knew who that was so they rushed around locking the doors and windows.

"Little Pig, Little Pig, let me come in," called the magic shark, growing upset.

"Oh no," answered the little pigs. "Not by the hairs on our chinny, chin, chins."

"You will be sorry!"
screamed the furious magic shark
in his loudest voice. "I will huff
and I will puff and I will blow
your house down." No one answered
and no one opened the door, so the
furious magic shark huffed and the
furious magic shark puffed and he
huffed and he puffed and he blew . . .

and nothing happened!

Again he huffed and he puffed and he huffed and he puffed and he blew and he blew and still nothing happened.

Once more the furious magic shark huffed and the furious magic shark puffed and the furious magic shark huffed and the furious magic shark puffed and the furious magic shark blew and blew and still . . . the lava rock house stood firm.

Now this made the magic shark extremely furious.
So, gathering up all of his air, the extremely furious
magic shark huffed and puffed

and huffed and puffed

and huffed and puffed

and

blew

and blew

and blew

and blew

and blew

and blew

and blew

until . . . whoosh; ker-splat,

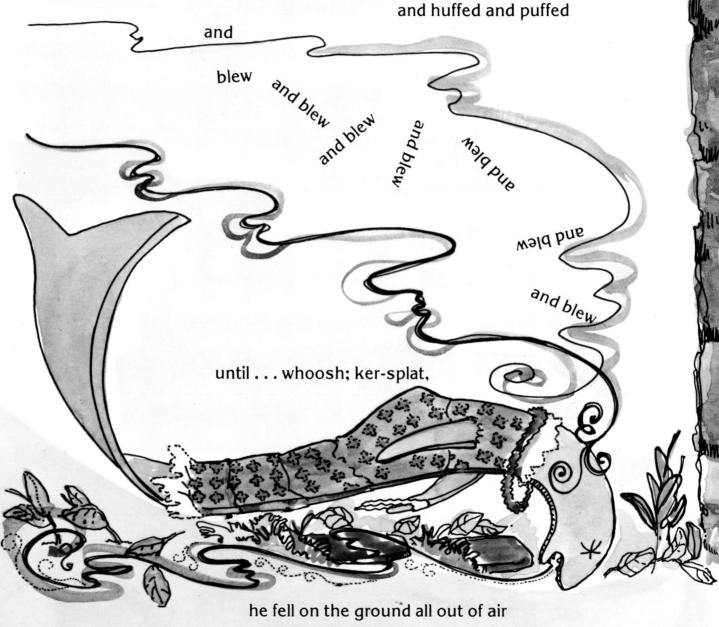

he fell on the ground all out of air
looking like a flat balloon!

It was quiet and still and the
three little pigs cautiously
peeked out of the house.
Seeing the very flat
magic shark, they
quickly ran outside,
rolled him up like
a straw mat, and
tied a string
around him. Then . . .

taking him off to the dump
they threw him away.

When they returned to the seashore, the third little pig helped his brothers build sturdy rock houses and once they were finished, the three little pigs gave a large party. They invited all their friends and relatives as well as a shave ice man (without a fin) to serve refreshments, a beachboy (without rows of sharp white teeth) to join the musicians, and a lei seller (without a shark's tail) to give out leis.

From then on the
three little pigs
lived safely and peacefully
beside the sea.

GLOSSARY

PUA'A a Hawaiian word meaning pig.

KEIKI what Hawaiians call a child.

ALOHA a Hawaiian word with meanings such as hello, goodbye, and love.

PILI GRASS a grass used to thatch grass houses in old Hawaii.

OPIHI a shallow, cone shaped limpet shell whose animal is prized eating.

LAVA rock formed by a volcano.

YELLOW TANG a small bright yellow reef fish.

HUMUHUMU a member of the trigger fish family; one of whom is the humuhumu-nukunuku-a-pua'a or fish with a snout like a pig, made famous in a popular Hawaiian song.

HE'E the Hawaiian word for octopus.

PUHI PAKA a ferocious eel with sharp teeth.

ULUA a kind of crevalle or jack fish.

OPAKAPAKA a blue snapper fish.

AHI a yellow fin tuna fish.

TRADE WINDS breezes which keep Hawaii cool.

SHAVE ICE powdery ice shavings put in a paper cone and covered with sweet, flavored syrup.

MUʻU MUʻU a long, loose fitting woman's dress.

UKULELE a four stringed instrument played by strumming, 'uke' is short for ukulele.

NOSE FLUTE a flute like instrument played by blowing air with the nose.

LEI a garland (usually of flowers)

LAU HALA leaf of the hala or Pandanus tree; used in weaving hats, rugs, and baskets.

PAU—FINISHED—PAU—ALL DONE—PAU—THE END!